For anyone who's ever left a shift smelling like grease.

Published by Stanchion Books, LLC

StanchionZine.com

Cover art by Jeff Bogle

ISBN: 979-8-88862-259-9

Irregulars

Kerry Trautman

STANCHION

I turned in my orders for tables 7 and 1. "Mr. Neery!" I yelled to Rusty, on the cooks' line. Most mornings, Rusty, his arms a flurry of flicking on switches, goes ahead and starts the banana pancakes as soon as he heats the grill, knowing Mr. Neery will be coming in promptly at 6:30. How sad that this little café is the one bright spot in Mr. Neery's life. His routine. He knows we have to be nice to him here.

I mean, this is my job—I get paid to be nice to people. That, and bring them eggs. I know Mr. Neery expects a smile, expects the table behind the hostess stand, with the view of the do-it-yourself carwash across Central Avenue, dimly barren at this hour of the morning. He expects the pancakes to taste the same as the day before, expects to see the brownish cigarette burn hole melted into the center of his vinyl tablecloth, which he fingers absentmindedly as he reads his Louis L'Amour novels. Expects us girls to work our usual shifts, and comments about it if we switch. And expects we'll chat with him about the latest Seinfeld episode.

As he enters the glass doors, he knows exactly how the next two hours will proceed. And all the time he's smiling like the smile's been tattooed on, like he can't stop, like the stronger he smiles, the stronger we will smile back. And he's right. Like philodendrons bending toward a southern window, we can't help but smile back. So I give him what he comes here for. Like a whore with a platter of banana pancakes, I smile and chitchat, and pat him on his bony shoulder, and for those two hours he sits, eats, smiles, and I'm his best friend in the world.

I get paid to be nice. But where can I go where someone has to be nice to me? Not a restaurant—the spell is broken. I know what waitresses are thinking about customers. I know the smiles are fake and they just want to get away from the table and relax their cheek and jaw muscles and do anything other than be nice to some stranger. People feel sorry for us waitresses because we wear insipidly-embroidered polyester aprons with our names on a plastic badge, because our skin sticks to our car seats as we drive home, and our hair smells like ham and cigarette smoke expelled from the bodies of dozens of strangers, because we have to play nice or we don't get paid.

But what they don't realize is there's something pathetic about customers too. Something about their hungry eyes as they watch each platter pass them to another table, thinking, "Ooh, here comes mine!" Then we walk on by, sort of satisfied to keep them hungry, keep them waiting their turn, like children. There's something sad about the fact that these people are not at home, with a mother or husband or wife making them breakfast in bed, or, damn it, doing it themselves. Or maybe that's just what we tell ourselves so we don't get pissed that they're spending ten bucks on bacon and juice, and pissed that we have to smile as we play accessory to their excess.

I gave Mr. Neery his banana pancakes, butter on the side, brown sugar in a little dish so he can sprinkle it in his coffee and mix it in with the butter to spread on the pancakes. No syrup. Maybe I'll try that sometime. I like to imagine it's something his mother taught him. That she'd grown up without fancy maple syrup, and this was what she'd learned to do, and after the Great War was over, and rations were lifted, she made him a big plate of pancakes with the luxury of butter and a sprinkle of brown sugar on top—just like she had when she was little. Hardly comfort for his father not making it home, but to a four-year-old boy, it was still a small taste of heaven. That's how I picture it anyway.

Mr. Neery drinks the coffee black until the food arrives, then with the sugar. It reminds me of the liquid fake sweetener my Grandpa used in his coffee—the clear glass jar was always on the kitchen table, and sometimes he'd let me drizzle it in because I liked the little drip-spout top. And he'd say "when" which meant I'd put in enough, and I never understood that as a kid. I smiled at Mr. Neery. He said, "Thank ya much," spread a napkin on his polyester plaid lap, proceeded to manipulate his sugar.

Table #7

Back in the kitchen, on the line, I had a fruit bowl and a pair of egg-white mushroom omelets for table 7. I buttered rye toast for one, wheat for the other, and carried them to the dining room.

"Here you are." I set Neal's plate in front of him. His wife, Nancy, had to move a few magazines and torn-out recipes from her place, her hot plate burning into my left thumb as I waited. These are the kind of folks who truly believe that some people, i.e. me, genuinely enjoy serving people. That noble waitresses, pool-boys, or gardeners derive pleasure from doing for others. Ridiculous. We just need money. And sometimes kissing-ass while performing tasks people are too lazy to perform themselves is the most easily attainable means to that end. Neal and Nancy aren't nasty people, just naive.

"Thank you, um…extra butter?" Neal's grey beard almost hid his kindly smile. His lips were very pink and moist. Nancy grimaced.

"Sure," I said, "be right back." He favors blazers—today's is forest green—and, as you can tell by his round belly, he refuses to exert himself. In my mind, Neal is a sculptor, and a realtor, and his tours of homes are more like leisurely strolls through a park. He points out the charming features of houses, especially older ones, with the pride of a parent describing his child's preschool artwork: "See how inspired that wood choice was, as it affects the overall color scheme." He wants the homebuyers to appreciate details as he does in his own house. Like the leaded-glass transom between the library and the living room—milky white except for a cobalt shape like a dove in flight in the center pane. Even if he doesn't look up, he smiles just walking under it. Such things are often lost on buyers, he fears, particularly on the younger ones who balk at a lack of closet space.

I try to imagine how Neal would soliloquize about my childhood home. "Note how the xanthic nicotine glow on the living room walls coordinates precisely with the concentric water stains on the ceiling," he would gush. "Oh, mind your shoes there—that's cat vomit. Blends perfectly with the vintage shag carpeting, doesn't it? Genius!"

"Here you are, sir." I brought the butter. I could see that table 3 needed me.

"Oh, and more coffee and…Tabasco maybe?" Neal said. I nodded and left. He watched Nancy poke at her fruit, removing a peach slice because, he supposed, it had a large, ribbed splotch of red in the center where the flesh had clung to the pit. He sipped his coffee, still chewing a bite of egg. "I finished that piece, I think, last night."

"Did you?" Nancy smiled.

"Yes. I'm happy with it. I don't think it needs anything more." He'd been working in his studio above the garage late into the night, which was unusual because he normally would begin working at dawn. Nancy had heard him come to bed at three a.m.

"Is it ready to show, you think?"

"Yes, I believe so," he said. Nancy reached over and patted his hand. He hated when she did that. Made him feel childish. "The boys coming for the show, you think?"

"Yes. They said they were, at least." After trying to conceive for their first three years of marriage, Nancy worried they'd end up being old parents. She had been a "surprise" for her parents, her sisters being eight and ten when she was born. She knew her parents loved her, but they were always exhausted. She remembers spending hours on her father's lap, being read-to and later practicing reading to him, while her sisters were doing homework. Nancy eventually became pregnant, and again the following year. Now the boys were away at college, neither studying art. Nancy curled a strand of sandy hair around her finger. "I can't wait to see the piece."

"I'll show you when we get home," Neal said. He loved her hair—that she let the few grays around her face stay natural, that she kept it long and loose and wavy instead of the middle-aged crop most women her age have. He never did know what she really thought about his sculptures—whether she truly liked them or was just trying to be supportive. He assumed she never could appreciate them as deeply as he did.

Nancy sighed dramatically as Neal spread butter on his toast. His cardiologist wanted him to be cautious until his bloodwork was re-checked. "You know, it'd probably taste fine without that." She immediately regretted speaking up.

"Damn it," he growled quietly, dropping his knife loudly to the plate and glaring downward. "Can't I just eat?"

Nancy remembered her father's funeral. "So young," the people muttered, though her father had always been an old man to her. Her third-grade teacher kept patting her shoulder whenever she came near, as if everything should be fine. Like saying, "Enough already, wake up." Adults at the funeral and at school smiled that tight little smile with a tilted head and said, "It'll be ok, you'll see," like she was just a plant that needed water, but still the sweet old man was gone. Nancy had grieved in that easy child's way—sobbing quietly into large grownup shoulders, taking long bike rides alone, swinging on her swingset while softly singing the comforting church hymns whose lovely words she didn't really understand yet knew by heart.

Maybe the kind of grieving I imagine for Nancy is less realistic than my own. When my dad died, I was twenty and had an opening shift at six the next morning. I had stayed at the hospital with my mom until midnight then slept on her Goodwill couch with two cats vying for a coveted position on my head. My mourning consisted of having a friend drive me to the reservoir—my one remembered outing with my father was fishing there—with a fifth of Smirnoff. Vodka is something sure to forever remind me of him.

I topped-off Neal and Nancy's coffees and nodded to table 3 so she would know I had seen her. I wanted to get away from Neal and Nancy. Wanted them to never come back. Wanted them and their two full-scholarship brats to go sit in that damn gallery and gape at some carved-up hunk of rock as if it had just shit mangos and fool themselves into thinking it was important, that it made them important.

"More cream, if you will?" Neal said, not looking up from forking his eggs. As I headed to the kitchen for cream, I smiled at Mrs. Finch at table 3 and showed her my notepad, so she'd know I was writing the ticket for her usual oatmeal. I thought how Neal and Nancy are so easy with one another. Know each other. Sure, they have their inner monologues that don't always seem to warrant sharing, but still they moved in sync, like a pair of oars dutifully guiding their mutual lifeboat to an agreed-upon shore.

My parents spun their marriage in sloppy circles, never bothering to fight the currents. I imagine my mom, after she dies —a quiet death, maybe in the hospital after a "routine" procedure like bunion removal, where dying simply involves an elevator ride from one floor to another. She wouldn't want the drama of a car crash, or collapsing from an aneurysm in Foodtown while reaching for a bag of frozen peas. So I imagine her in heaven or, more likely, the mother-of-pearly gates of purgatory, where she is reunited with my dad. He'd glance up from the fishing channel and say, "So how was it for you?"

"Didn't feel a thing," she'd say. And he'd assume she'd meant her death, but the rest of us would know she'd been referring to her life.

Table #2

Entering the kitchen with table 7's empty cream pitcher, I felt a sticky spot near the edge of the slatted swinging door. Thought I should remember to wipe it later.

Lisa was leaning against the Coke machine, re-writing a sloppy ticket before turning it in. "Rusty's pretty good at interpreting our writing," I offered, turning in a ticket for table 3. Lisa was new, and always worried about pissing off the cooks. They loved it—sensing fear, knowing we're at their mercy and that our tips are directly linked to their speed and skill.

"I know," she said, "I just don't need to mess-up so soon." I wanted to ask her to braid her over-long, stuck-in-high-school hair so she wouldn't shed all over the kitchen.

"It happens," I said. I grabbed a towel from the sanitizer bucket, wiped down the swinging door, re-filled the cream for 7.

Lisa turned-in her ticket and began cleaning the nozzles of the Coke machine, sanitizing the spouts, wiping the under-counter maze of sticky tubes. I remembered visiting my father in the hospital—gawking at the limp slab of flesh, distended belly rising in irregular, twitchy swells, the color-coded tubes flowing with fluids of varying shades of clear, invading every orifice and creating new ones of their own. Instantly I had begun mourning —not the loss of that bloated, flawed man, but the loss of what he had never magically changed into, never been capable of, never allowed me to have.

Sandi and Meg breezed in from the back door, tying their aprons.

"So I was like so hammered and he was so awesome at that guitar and he never even had like lessons or anything so later I was like letting him feel me up and stuff..." Sandi yammered as they punched in.

"We all knew," Meg said. "I mean you guys were in the bathroom for like ever." They giggled and studied the seating chart with their assigned sections. Meg looked at me. "You totally should have come last night. Good times." They headed out to the dining room. I followed with cream for 7 and napkins and syrup for 2.

I've gone out with the girls from work a couple of times, but I hate the pressure of being friends with them all. As if it's some kind of sorority where we sling eggs by day and pound daiquiris by night. It's odd how getting drunk is such a bonding experience to some people. As if someone who gives you a stick of Trident after you puke is instantly akin to your long-lost sister. In the end it wouldn't matter how many parties we'd go to or pizzas we'd share, we'd still just be "work friends"— that messy, half-breed category of sub-par relationships where you never know if they genuinely like you or are just trying to stay on your good side so you'll swap shifts when they need to. One day they're helping you hook up with a drummer, the next day they're bitching to the manager that you slacked on your sidework. I remain cordial, but I don't come to work to make friends—I come to make money.

Besides, I never have felt comfortable getting to know people, small-talk stuff. I sometimes imagine I'm talking through a sheet of plexi-glass. Or my body is wrapped in a coating of cellophane. No one else can really see it's there, but still I think I filter my world through it. Heat is less warm through my plastic. Water less wet.

I brought the cream pitcher to 7 and napkins and syrup to the woman, Sue, at 2. She gave napkins to her two little boys who were busy coloring dot-to-dots of sunny-side eggs on their paper placemats. "Here, let's make room for your plates," she said to them. "They'll be here soon." Sue slid drippy milk glasses and balled-up straw wrappers to the center of the table, carefully aligning each boy's glass with the middle of his placemat. She liked them to feel even.

When the boys were babies, three months old, she took them to the mall—her first real outing just for fun, just to show them off to the world in all their drooly-chinned, blubbery-

cheeked glory. It had been the ordeal she'd imagined it might be
—packing spare clothes for both in case they wet through,
packing their favorite cow-shaped rattle to shake in front of their
faces if they fussed in their stroller, pacifiers, bottles, bibs to
absorb their drool and not ruin their cute, matching outfits
chosen to garner "oohs" and "how sweets" from mall-walking
strangers. The last thing she wanted was to get to the mall,
fumble with the double-seater stroller, lug the babies inside, and
realize she'd forgotten something essential. She didn't want
some woman glaring at her like she's some charity case,
thinking, "now why doesn't that girl have a blanket over those
poor babies? Doesn't she know malls always turn the air
conditioning too high?"

But on that day Sue had remembered everything she
needed, and the boys were in a particularly good mood. She'd
made a pleasant lap around the mall, enjoying the admiring
gazes of its patrons toward her lovely little twins. After a half-
hour or so she went into the ladies' room, finding that the only
stalls that would fit her and the huge stroller were the stalls
marked with the blue "handicapped" sign. She didn't want to
take up one of them, fearing some wheelchair-bound woman
might enter and be put out. So instead Sue used a smaller stall,
leaving the stroller just outside its closed door, wheels visible
underneath. The restroom was quiet, and she listened for the
stirrings and cooing of the boys. She watched for strange shoes
to approach the stroller; none did.

Then, as Sue was fumbling to button her jeans—still too
tight but she'd tried to wear them anyways because they were

nicer than the size-up pair that truly fit her—a pair of pink
sneakers appeared.

"Well hi there," the voice of the sneakers-wearer said
flatly, and softly, as though no one was listening.

Sue's heartbeat quickened and she dove for the door
lock, trying to open it as quickly yet gracefully as she could. She
didn't want to offend some sweet old lady or curious child. But
she wanted those boys in her sight as quickly as possible. "I'm
right here, boys!" She almost-shouted, cheerfully, the door
swinging open to reveal a middle-aged woman standing, bent
forward, near the stroller. As soon as she saw Sue, the woman
stood upright, nodded silently with a bland smile, and slipped
into a stall, locking it. The boys were calm. Alan, in the front
seat of the two, smiled at her.

But why was the woman bent over? To see them better?
Or, no, Sue swore she saw the woman's hand reaching toward
the stroller. To what—simply squeeze his flabby cheeks or tickle
his toes? Or . . . To unbuckle him and run away with him? Sue's
head throbbed and she shoved the stroller out of the ladies' room
as quickly as it would go. "I'm being silly," she thought,
straining to hold the heavy door open. But as she left she
glanced back to see that the sneakers-wearer had yet to drop her
pants, the shoes poised just behind the stall door.

As Sue looked for her car in the lot, she cried. She felt
like a failure as a mother for having let the babies out of her
sight in a strange place. She envisioned all those TV crime
investigation shows, and the six-o'clock news: story after story

of missing, stolen, murdered children. And here she was, leaving her babies out of reach in a public bathroom.

She felt particularly guilty about Alan having been in the front seat—the more vulnerable position, the first to enter whatever danger lie ahead, the most easily coughed-on or bumped-into by strangers—and she hugged him tightly as she put him into the car, whispering "I'm sorry so so sorry" into her kisses on his cheeks. After that day, she rotated which boy would have to sit in the front position, saying a silent prayer as she'd buckle him in. She didn't want one to feel preferred, one to feel neglected, even for a moment.

Driving home Sue passed a home with a plastic banner hanging across its front door, proclaiming, "It's a Girl!" in pink lettering. "You fools," Sue thought. "Why announce your vulnerability to the world? Looking for a baby to steal? Here's one! Right here behind these thin walls of glass and wood, easily penetrated by anyone willing to try."

Now, Sue accepted the two platters of chocolate-chip waffles I brought out for her. She cut them into small pieces, placed them in front of her boys. "Need anything else?" I asked. Sue shook her head. She seemed irritated by my presence. She didn't want anyone disrupting her time with her sons.

I wondered how I would have reacted to a situation like the one Sue faced. I feel like I'm pretty well-prepared to feel fear. I expect it. Anticipate it, for instance in a dark parking lot, or a thunderstorm, or when a date is walking me to my door. In such situations I'm constantly on edge, thinking at any minute something's going to happen to scare the hell out of me; it never does.

When I was a kid, I always thought nightmares were God's way of preparing me for danger in the future. Like field training for impending battle. Grown-ups tell you to forget the nightmares, put them out of your head, but that doesn't make sense. How else is a kid supposed to become aware of, and practice being faced with danger, with evil? Whenever I awoke, upended in my small bed, tiny heart racing like a handful of marbles down the cellar stairs, I tried to commit the nightmare to memory. Monster in the basement … silvery fur … orange glowing eyeballs … in the basement … oh, Grandma's basement, yes … and there's a window … the monster's blocking the stairs, but there's a window … it's small, but so am I … yes, I have it … remember the window.

I went to the kitchen for the coffee pots to make the rounds. Behind the line, Rusty was grumbling at Lisa. "You didn't write 'well-done.' How was I supposed to know you wanted 'well-done?' I ain't some kinda mind-reader." He slid one of Lisa's plates under the broiler while she swallowed back tears. Rusty continued grumbling under his breath as he worked.

I grimaced, thinking of Sue doting on her boys. My parents always told us that growing up poor developed character. As if they were broke on purpose for our benefit. But if I had grown up rich, then living as I do now would make me pissed-off all the time, constantly thinking back to the good old days of family dinners out, private lessons, a wardrobe of shoes. This way, there's nowhere to go but up. Some guy would be lucky to have me for a wife; I'm easily impressed.

Lisa rolled her eyes at me and I tried to give her a sympathetic look. I could tell she needs an ally around here, especially when Rusty's in one of his moods. I thought about giving her some advice: always start-off self-deprecating, like "Rusty I am such an idiot, I needed this well-done but didn't write it. Help me please!" Make the cooks feel like they're in control—which they are, really, because if the food sucks your tip does too. Another tactic I could have detailed for Lisa is to blame the customer. "Rusty, you cooked this absolutely *perfectly* and that jerk wants it well-done. Can you believe it! Could you slip it under the broiler for him?" Lisa will learn those kinds of things over time. How to lie, be an actress, whatever gets you what you need.

Table #4

The man alone at table 4 had nearly finished his omelet, and I refilled his decaf. He was good-looking, but I knew better than to ask a regular out. Flirt just enough to keep them in a good mood, but dating is bad news. The ketchup mess on Jay's plate reminded me of my father, who put ketchup on everything —fried chicken, nachos, ham sandwiches. Jay didn't look up as he mumbled "thanks." He was studying his nude ring finger, stroking its soft underbelly with a fingertip of his right hand.

"Four months," Jay thought, "four." The day before, he'd driven past River's Edge Park and saw the river had flooded, which was odd for so late in June. The chains for the swings disappeared under the brown water like twinned anchors. Picnic tables floated around the shelter houses, and he imagined them, as the waters receded, drifting and landing where they will, like lost souls of a shipwreck settling to the ocean floor.

Passing the park, he remembered how he'd proposed there. April had sat on a warped wooden bench overlooking the small waterfall. He waded calf-deep, ten yards or so out into the gurgling water, striated from rocks under the surface. He thought, if April had been wearing a skirt he'd have a perfect view up under it from here, but she wore jeans, so his eyes focused instead on a large pink blob of gum adhered to the underside of the bench. Jay got down on his knee and shouted back, "April, will you marry me?"

A fisherman on the opposite bank called out, "Say yes!"

Now with the flood, it seemed as if the whole scene had been swallowed back into the water and drained away.

They had settled into their marriage easily, despite having only known each other three months. Jay, at age twenty, had been a virgin. April wasn't, and he felt like her fingertips created new nerve-endings in his skin. He became insatiable. He wanted her several times a day, in every room in the apartment, on every piece of furniture, strip of countertop, or floor. He bought videos to re-enact, and a camera to record themselves— which she refused, and they fought about it. "You're like some crazed teenager!" she accused. "Grow up!"

But Jay thought this must be what it means to be an adult —taking charge of your body and confidently seeking out what you need, providing for your own desires. He wasn't a kid anymore, jerking-off in long showers, freezing up if he thought he heard footsteps in the hall. Sex was real, and a perpetual option. He began to sexualize everyone he saw. He imagined the cashier at the supermarket bent over the check-line, the pimply bagger-boy taking her from behind, her cheek mashed against the scrolling black grocery belt. Sitting in a darkened movie theater, he pictured the crowd erupting in a giant groping orgy— buttery popcorn fingers sliding over and in and out of one another's bodies, women draped over the red velour chairs, Dolby sound still blaring—trying to mentally will it to happen, practically *expecting* it to happen. But what he most wanted was to bring home other women to join him and his wife.

One night, at a bar with April, they'd chatted with an attractive woman. April seemed to get along with her, so Jay decided to take that as a go-ahead, and he got her phone number. The next night, when April came home from shopping, Jay led her to the bedroom where the woman waited, sprawled on their bed in just her green panties reading their TV Guide. April screamed, thinking he was having an affair, screamed again when he told her what he had planned, and she locked herself in the bathroom.

The next day, after four months of marriage, Jay arrived home from work to find her gone, every sign of her missing from their apartment. She even took their wedding album, which he, guiltily, didn't even realize until weeks later. She took everything they'd been given as wedding gifts—every last platter, goblet, and pepper mill. It was as though he'd imagined her.

So he tried to put her out of his mind, went back to jerking-off in long showers, no one to interrupt. Hell, he didn't even need the cover of a shower anymore. He could do it right in the living room while watching porn at full volume. But he was surprised that it just wasn't the same. He missed *her*, not just the sex.

He finds, when he cooks, he makes enough food for both of them, just in case she suddenly appears at the door one night. Then after he eats, standing at the kitchen counter, he saves the leftovers—stuffing the spaghetti, or tuna sandwich, or whatever it is into a plastic baggie and stashing it in the freezer. Like a triumph over decay, he suspends the food's viability in time. Yet every time he opens the precariously stuffed freezer he is reminded, usually with a bruise to the top of the foot, of all that he has been unable to finish.

I brought him his check and he sighed when he saw written on it that he was at table 4. "Four months," he muttered.

"Excuse me?" I said.

"Nothing, I …" He stopped. I felt, for some reason, that I shouldn't leave his side. Had to stop myself from putting my hand on his shoulder. He looked up at me, my eyes. "I'm fine," he smiled thinly. "Could I have a box for the rest?" He handed me his plate with a small island of coagulated omelet surrounded by a smear of ketchup.

I dropped my eyes from him and hurried to the kitchen. I wanted to tell him that he was lucky his marriage ended as soon as it did—imagine how much worse he'd feel if she left ten years down the line, taking their three kids with her. I wanted to tell him that now he's better prepared to communicate with a new woman. Wanted to tell him that I was sorry his soul throbbed every time he opened the door to the dark apartment that still smelled like her shampoo. To tell him that I use the same brand. Tell him that I don't cook much, but I love leftovers. That I'm free tonight. But I had people waiting.

Table #5

On my way to the kitchen, Sandi told me she'd sat me a doozy of a table. I brought coffee pots to table 5. "Coffee?" I asked them.

"Thank you," they all said simultaneously, smiling. Triplet girls, thirty-years old, blond. They were average-looking individually, but somehow viewed all together they were stunning. The way one tiny blue light might seem nice, but strung together and hung on a pine tree they're spectacular. Greater impact. I poured the coffee, noticed their cream was empty, and went to refill it. What was odd was that they still dressed alike—jeans and the same style blouse but in different colors. Matching heavy, beaded bracelets.

Jennifer has always been the blue girl, which pleased her father because, since he had no son, at least there was some blue in the house along with the ruffles and flowers and pink pink pink. Why did people always give pink gifts to baby girls? There are so many other ways to show femininity. So Jennifer's dresses and jammies and barrettes were blue. Occasionally she'd have to wear boy clothes thinly disguised as girls'. Their mother would sew a daisy appliqué over top of a choo-choo on a blue t-shirt, as if no one could tell. At age four, Jennifer told the other girls they can't wear jeans because jeans are blue, and their mom had to explain that jeans are neutral, universal. Jennifer, therefore, had to share blue with her sisters, which she resented. And she has to share her blue with the rest of the world too because jeans, of course, are everywhere. She stays away from shopping malls. Facing a crowd of jeans-legs strolling past her at all angles makes her furious, and lonely. As if all those denim asses exist merely to remind her that she is, ultimately, just one of many. She never will be unique.

Janice is the pink girl. Usually their mom tried to find outfits that came in all three colors so it'd be exactly the same for each girl, but invariably Janice ended up with more clothes. Prettier ones. She got all the dresses her mom "couldn't resist" or gifts from acquaintances that were unaware of the system. She liked to dress in her mother's clothes whenever she could. Her world was full of possibilities. She became interested in theater in high-school, and got to play Stella in Streetcar when she was only a freshman—pissed off a lot of seniors. When they were little, their father sometimes called Janice "too big for her britches." Jennifer never knew what britches were, but she liked to hear her father say it.

Jane is the purple girl. This was decided because she was born in the middle. A combination of blue and pink. She could side with either sister according to her convenience. When

Jennifer needed a witness to tattle on Janice for pulling the head off Malibu Barbie, Jane would do so. But Jane would later swipe one of Jennifer's Oreos after dinner, saying, "Hey, I helped *you*!" When Janice needed an alibi to sneak to the movies with Greg Kramer, Jane told their parents Janice was at the mall with her, but Janice had to promise to ask Greg's friend Bill to call Jane. Jane is resourceful. She decorates her apartment with a lot of purple—she truly likes it—and she is always aware of which shades lean more toward red and which are more bluish. If Jennifer comes over, Jane worries that she might be insulted if she notices, for instance, that the purple wine glasses are decidedly more pinkish. Jane will then be sure to use her purple napkins, because they really are almost periwinkle. She wouldn't want Jennifer to get the wrong idea.

I returned to table 5 to take orders—four stacks of pancakes. Their mother had joined them. Dressing alike now, as adults, is to please their mother. She had put so much energy into staging the triplets, they feel they owe it to her to continue. They assume their identities like superheroes slipping on their colored capes, temporarily disregarding their normal selves. Their mom can see, in their color-coded bracelets, the fruits of her years of labor jangling back at her. The girls think they're fooling everyone, disguised as a perfect unit. But I know all about disguises.

I turned in the order, grabbed plates for 2, syrup for 5, noticed the busser had cleared 4. I dropped plates at 2, syrup at 5. The triplets all took their coffee light. We actually have good coffee here, so black is best. My mom taught me to take it black. To sip slowly and with a lot of air, like wine. To drench your tongue. To respect it. To take it seriously.

Mom tends to ritualize things. Every holiday dinner with extended family is planned weeks in advance—from the candles, to the tablecloth, to the music she'll play on an old cassette player that plays slightly too fast so the songs all seem to be in too-high a key. She assumes her sisters from out-of-town will notice how the ribbon she tied on to the garage-sale chandelier matches the one they'd passed on the front door wreath, instead of noticing the nine-inch hole in the plaster of the dining room wall in front of which she'd strategically placed a potted plant. They'll notice that she'd "coordinated" all of the plants by painting their plastic pots the same dingy off-white as the walls, instead of noticing that the rickety table shakes when we all cut our meat, sloshing the unused, unnecessary water glasses. Never mind that the cats will invade our laps in search of handouts, their hair ending up on plates even fresh from the dishwasher, hair traveling home with each guest on their clothing, like barnacles spreading port to port on hulls of barges.

Mom has the Family Meal planned in her head. So when one of us sits in something other than our pre-determined chair, or a child won't try the squash, or my older sister burps, or when dad tells a joke involving the Pope, a Rabbi, and a whore, Mom rolls her eyes, tightens her lips, pretends it's some other family, in some other house, that ruins every perfect meal.

Table #3

As I walked past table 3 I realized Mrs. Finch's oatmeal should be ready by now. I went to the kitchen. "Rusty," I yelled, "got oatmeal for 3 yet?"

"Shit," he muttered, scooping overdone, too-thick oatmeal from pot to bowl. He added a little extra hot water and stirred. "Good as new." He slid the bowl over the line to me.

"Thanks." I brought it out to the table. Agnes Finch comes in twice a week, alone. She knits or reads while she sips cinnamon tea and eats oatmeal. "Here you are, Mrs. Finch. Need another teabag?"

"In a bit, honey," she smiled. Agnes loves birds, and was thrilled to acquire the name "Finch" when she married Donald. They'd met at Marblehead Park on Lake Erie when she was fourteen. He was eighteen, in the Army, on his way to Germany the next day. Agnes was feeding stale rolls to some gulls when she saw him gazing out at the lake in his white uniform, stepping gingerly along the precarious limestone ridges at the shoreline. She thought if he had been a beautiful woman his hair would be whipping wildly, body bending in the breeze. But instead, his body seemed so solid—strong and reliable as the lighthouse looming behind him. She hoped he'd see her there on the stone bench, with the hollyhocks and bachelor's buttons that she knew looked so pretty growing behind her. She smoothed her dress, gathered her hair into a yellow scarf from her pocket, waiting for him to turn towards her.

He wrote to her from the front, and they were married when he returned, eight months later, with shrapnel lodged in his left thigh. When he died she brought his ashes back to Marblehead and buried them near the bench, along with hollyhock seeds to replace the ones long since spent. She threw crumbs into the wind when the gulls appeared, hoped some wrens or jays might come after she'd gone.

I don't know why I romanticize couples in love years and years ago. As if there weren't horny assholes in the 1930s. As if there weren't women clambering into the laps of any strange man who would buy them a Rob Roy. As if men never lied, never beat their women, and all babies born had the daddies their mamas said they had. I assign to old people an innocent past full of promise and naïveté. Maybe it's because if I assume sweetness and purity really once existed I can hang onto the hope that it can be resurrected. I need to believe I'm descendant from women like Agnes.

Now, on Mondays and Thursdays, Agnes's nurse from the Glenwood Home brings her to the café, helps her in, and returns for her two hours later. At Glenwood, Agnes loves the birdcage in the south lounge. The lounge has rattan furniture, the sofa cushions patterned with palm fronds and tiny blue and gold monkeys swinging from curling vines. There is a ten-foot long aviary busy with the flutterings of songbirds hopping between branches, and seed treats.

Agnes spends hours watching the birds and can't understand why people seem to look at her like she's crazy when she describes the birds' comings and goings, explains their relationships to one another—that the green parakeet is jealous of the blue one's longer tail and he hops away whenever Bluey comes near, or that the goldfinch prefers to peck the chrome bell while the yellow warbler only rings the gold bell. Why do the nurses seem to think she makes up this information? Why don't they find it fascinating? Why don't they see that without the bird society in the south lounge, and without the feeders in the courtyard that especially attract winter cardinals, without the tiny black eyes—blank of anything but sweetness—and tiny wire feet, without their predictable feathery interactions she would have nothing, nothing to look forward to most days?

Agnes also enjoys her days at the café. She smiles deeply in her eyes at every child that passes by her, and always wants a seat near a window. I brought Agnes a teabag and a fresh hot water pot. Her knitted scarf was coming along nicely.

I couldn't imagine my mother knitting. Too big of a commitment. Once she'd start a sweater or something, the unfinished project would loom over her, a nagging burden in her mind, the needles clinking in her dreams, the yarn twisting itself together in her mind as she drove to the store, paid bills, changed the litter box. When she'd finally finished the sweater —dug through her closet for a matching skirt and earrings, wore it to work so if anyone complimented her on it she could say, proudly, that she'd made it herself—when she finally reached the point where it was totally hers, she would hate it. It would become like the book you wrote your senior thesis on and you never want to read again, having turned it inside out in your brain, memorized it, drained it of all joy.

I went to the kitchen for plates for 5, saw one for 8 too. "Want me to take this to 8 for you?" Sandi offered.

"I'll be right back," I said. Sandi always prattles on and on about her fiancé. The rest of know he'll never marry her, never even get her the ring he's been "shopping for" for two years. Still she clings to his "I could see us getting married some day" as an elegant proposal and she started saying "fiancé." I delivered to 5, came back for the plate for 8. Sandi was telling Lisa the story of how she met her boyfriend while Lisa filled a tray of saltshakers. Sandi loves that story. He was a waiter at another table near hers at a Mexican restaurant where she was celebrating her mom's birthday with her extended family. All the waiters gathered to sing some absurd clappity-clapclap birthday song around the table, and he couldn't take his eyes off her. He sent a free pitcher of margaritas to the table with his number on a napkin. Sandi's always suggesting I go out with her and her fiancé again sometime, but I'd hate to tell her what a dolt I think he is. She seems to like Lisa pretty well.

I did hang out with them once. And Meg too. We all went camping in a forested state park edged on two sides by a bay. It was nice being secluded with the woosh of waves gentle behind the rustle of leaves. I don't drink often, not since my older sister was arrested for being found wandering, drunk, down the middle of the street. Usually she just drank at a friend's house or in the back yard. But it scared me to think that she couldn't control herself, that she'd end up like Dad.

And what scared me more was that Mom didn't get mad. She just picked her up, silent, and drove her home, me in the front seat of the brown Chevy wagon. I remember how cramped the car felt on that drive home, and how Mom never even looked us in the eyes. I remember thinking how Aunt Bess once mentioned that Mom was "right wild" when she was a teenager, back in West Virginia. I liked the image of Mom hiking up mountainsides—alone or maybe with a boy—camping under moonlight, or canoeing down a river, long hair whipping.

Camping that night with Sandi and Meg, drinking beers and eating hot dogs right off sizzling sticks, I'd felt like I wanted to be safe and wild at the same time. I poked at the fire with a long stick, stirring the embers, thought about how fire grows, what feeds it. It needed the same things I do—air, food, and space to grow, spread. Flecks of gleaming ash swirled up from the flames, disappearing into the black above. I wondered where they would land, wondered what it would feel like to flicker and fly away, a fading light in the sky.

Table #8

I grimaced inside as I approached table 8. A homely girl, by herself, was engrossed in her meal. The skin of her face was planetary, like the satellite image of some newly-discovered cosmic body that would be called, by a NASA spokesperson on CNN, "inhospitable." She pierced an over-easy yolk with her toast, smeared the bread 'til it dripped with the yellow ooze, lifted the mess to her pimply face, a flap of egg white flopping over the edge of the crust like a catfish twitching, gasping on a pier.

The girl reminded me of a time my boyfriend and I went to Dunkin' Donuts and an acne-faced clerk strolled up to the case. She plopped her hand onto the glass top, like a troll suspicious that visitors might steal her precious jewels. "Whatcha want?" the girl asked, her temples and furry upper-lip perspiring. I considered the donuts, and the unsettling proximity of the sweaty clerk to them. Waiting, the clerk lifted the rumpled skirt of her dingy white apron and wiped it across her lumpy face, exhaling wetly. She let the apron drop then proceeded to wipe her hands thoroughly on it. "Decide yet?"

I unconsciously lifted my hand to my mouth, imagining the rough canvas apron rupturing the clerk's many inflamed pimples, releasing their creamy insides onto the fabric, her moist fingers now smeared with the pus along with traces of powdered sugar and maple glaze. "N-nothing," I stammered, backing away. "Uh, never mind." My boyfriend, now confused, had not seen the wiping, as he was deep in donut-choosing concentration. Later, I had to look away as he, humming, devoured his Boston cream.

Standing at table 8, I couldn't bring myself to look the girl in the face as I asked, "How is everything?" I was sure there would be egg yolk oozing from the corners of her slack, chewing mouth.

"Ketchup," the girl said moistly, and I turned away, but that reminded me that table 7 had asked me for Tabasco and I'd forgotten to drop it off. I stopped by and produced the bottle from my pocket, but they were pretty much done so I was too late and felt stupid. I could hear the girl at 8 chewing, repeatedly scraping her plate with her fork.

I went for the ketchup, and there was a clatter of plates from the dish room.

"Shitdamnshit!" I heard the disher yell. I don't know where my boss finds these people, but our dishers are never exactly socially adept. This particular guy disappears into the employee restroom for a half-hour after every shift to take some sort of sponge bath in the sink. He emerges with slicked hair and a new outfit, the day's work clothes stuffed in a red plastic tackle box. We waitresses have—affectionately, of course—named him "Bubbles," partly because of the foamy mountain left in restroom sink after his cleansing ritual, and partly because he brings in his own bottles of liquid dish soap by the caseload to supplement the required, Health Department-approved, detergent in the dish machine which, consequently, requires an extra rinse cycle. Of course, I guess someone who chooses to be a disher must not have had too many career options lined up.

I hate the dish room. Our boss made each waitress spend a shift in there to see what it's like. It sucks—big surprise. It's not that I mind getting dirty—which you do, very dirty—it's just so monotonous. The same egg yolk smears, bacon grease, and hash brown detritus. Sugar packet wrappers and wilted lettuce leaf garnishes glued to the plate with syrup or hollandaise. Napkins wadded into mugs by some toddler whose mom let him play to shut him up. Not to mention the mountains of wasted food. People pay six bucks for a quarter's-worth of eggs, then throw out half. It's nauseating—or maybe that's just the smell of the grease trap. And it doesn't help to have Bubbles telling you dirty jokes, dropping a rack of saucers from his sudsy hands, shouting "Damnfuckerfuckershitdamn!" then berating you for dropping a fork in the spoon slot.

If it was just me in there, the one thing to enjoy about the dish room would be the solitude. No watching people chew their bite of food before they respond to your basically-rhetorical question: "How is everything?" No waiting for people to finish a cell-phone conversation after they've summoned you to their table to take their order. No being called sweetheart by men in Ray-Bans. No strained smiles. Alone in the dish room you just go about your required duties in peace, you cleanse what once was filthy, bring order to chaos tray by tray, quietly make a vile greasy mess of yourself, then go home for a gratifying hot shower.

Out on the floor there's the same monotony of coming in to work, making a big mess, cleaning it all up at the end of the day, then coming in the next day to mess it all up again. But in the dish room, the purity of those trays of sparkling glasses and pristine white plates keeps you motivated. You feel like you are constantly succeeding, constantly producing something beneficial, doing good. And because we have only just enough of everything, the bussers are always happy to take the clean trays away, smiling, "Oh, silverware! You're awesome!"

Table #9

I brought ketchup to the girl at table 8 without looking at her, and brought a bottle to table 9 also. I did look at these two guys, and they had not, in fact, asked for the ketchup, but I'd brought it as an excuse to look at the tall one again. He looked haggard, enveloping his coffee cup with both big hands. "How are the omelets?" I asked, smiling.

"Oh, fine." Dan answered, letting go of the mug, sitting back.

"More coffee here, please," said Craig, the shorter of the two.

"Rough night?" I ventured. Dan's eyes darted up to mine then back down, as if he'd been caught looking down the front of my shirt, a pink flush spreading up his neck to his earlobes. Craig laughed, and I left for the coffee pots, feeling I'd touched a nerve.

Dan and Craig had been to visit a mutual friend at The University of Dayton. Dan had come down a day earlier to stay a night with his cousin in Kettering. Later, the guys left UD in their separate cars and headed back here to Toledo, calling each other every once in a while to suggest radio stations—"Dude, 92.5, I dig this tune,"—and keep each other company. They stayed together as best they could, but they got separated in some construction traffic in Findlay, just as the sun was setting. Dan slid The Joshua Tree in the CD player and called Craig.

"I'm coming up on exit …167. How far back are you?"

"Couple miles," Craig said. "I'm getting hungry. Wanna stop?"

Dan felt like Craig was in the seat next to him. Like he'd reach over and turn up the stereo. "Yeah, but I'd kind of like to just get home."

"All right. Dude, I'm putting that disk in too. Later," Craig said. They hung up. Dan dropped his phone into the empty front seat, and looked up to see brake lights in front of him. Everyone braking. Dan slammed his brake pedal and skidded slightly into the grass on the right to avoid hitting the Camry in front of him. He braced himself, worrying the car behind him might hit. He sat for a few minutes, glad there'd been no crashes, and waited for traffic to move. It didn't. Figuring something happened up ahead, he cut off the engine and pulled out the pack of cigarettes he'd bought for this trip. He rarely smoked unless he was drinking.

The night was warm with a warm breeze and dusty, weedy smell of the newly-mown grassy median. Crickets trilled, accompanied by the intermittent whoosh of southbound traffic. The pavement was eerily still and very dark, now that all the northbound cars had given up and parked. Dan got out and lit a cigarette—didn't want the car to stink like smoke. He brushed the creases out of his shirt, the front of his pants. He thought cars should come with a tiny, cigarette-lighter-powered iron to undo the damage of a seatbelt.

Dan noticed a Ford startlingly close behind him, a girl sitting against the bumper. A beautiful, sweet-looking girl. A most fortunate development, since they were all stuck. "Smoke?" he held the pack out towards her.

"No," she sighed. "Quit."

"Shame." He pulled on his, felt a twinge guilty now, futilely blowing away from her over his right shoulder. His phone rang in the car. He ducked in, saw on the display it was Craig, answered. "What's up? You OK?"

"Yeah. Sucks though."

"Yeah, I know. Listen, can I call you back though?" Dan tried to keep his voice low. "There's this girl here…" He peeked out the back window at her, her hair blowing around her shoulders.

"Whatever, dude." Craig laughed. "Like what, you gonna nail her in the median or something?"

"Later." Dan stood, slid the phone in his pocket. "I'm Dan," he said, stepping towards her and extending his hand.

"Angela." She smiled. No one called her Angela but her parents, but it somehow seemed better than Angie. She was embarrassed of her old Escort, and wondered if she'd care about the car if this stranger wasn't so good-looking. She was supposed to get home. Angela decided, without even realizing she'd decided, not to tell him she had a daughter, hoping he wouldn't notice the empty baby seat in the back of her Escort. She felt good being just a pretty girl in the moonlight, instead of a single-mom college-dropout. She tugged at the hem of her t-shirt, to stretch it looser around her soft belly.

Dan sat against the back of his car, hoping he wouldn't get his pants dirty. Angela smoothed her hair, windblown from driving, wet her lips, looked side to side, thinking she'd never sit in the dark with a strange man except there were so many other cars around. If he tried to stab or rape her she could run. Everyone was out of their cars now with their cell phones. She felt safe. She wanted to smoke.

"Looks like we're not moving soon," Dan said, looking her body up and down as subtly as he could while pretending to gaze at the line of traffic beyond her. Up ahead, two kids were twirling sparklers in the median. Someone's radio played faintly.

"Yeah." She tried not to look worried, tried to enjoy the breeze, the soothing roar of the semis. It felt good to stretch her legs. "Where you headed?"

"Toledo. Visited a friend in Dayton." Dan nodded southward, shifted his weight, stepped a few inches closer. "You?"

"Just home. Not much farther, really." She thought how she could probably drive along the shoulder to her exit, the next one ahead, but she didn't want to risk getting a ticket. Besides, it was nice to have a chance to relax and talk to a guy. The old lady didn't even expect her home until morning, and surely she had the baby down by now and was asleep herself. She might as well stay put.

"Oh. Here," he said, pulling a business card from his pocket. "I just had these made. Need to give them to someone."

"Graphic designer," she read the embossed lettering, smiling. "I'll keep that in mind." She slid it in the back pocket of her jeans. They talked for a half-hour or so, leaning on their cooling cars. They learned from the chain of drivers in front of them, like a child's game of Telephone, that a semi had overturned ahead, spilling packages of frozen chicken, and crews had to be called to clean up. They were stuck for a few hours at least.

It's odd how a situation like that can suspend time. Like a power outage, or a fire drill at work. Of course there are better things to do with your time, but instead of dwelling on the wasted moments you allow yourself a short vacation from your life and just enjoy the unexpected diversion for what it is. Dan didn't worry about Craig, didn't think about what time he had to get up the next morning. Angela knew the baby was safe with the farmer's wife, didn't worry about the laundry piled up at home or the squeaky front-door hinge that needed WD-40. They just talked to each other.

Dan found it difficult to look away from Angela's eyes. They reflected the sparse, gold-ish streetlamps with a steady shine, even when occasionally glancing shyly downward. They felt familiar to him. Like the eyes of a favorite cousin who you played with as a child but rarely see as an adult, someone who, even so, seems to have memorized your personality, your cadence of speech, so that speaking to them is like speaking to yourself—even if it's a version of yourself you haven't seen in years.

Angela thought Dan seemed confident, someone unfazed by a challenge—like a flat tire, or getting fired, or a baby. But he had such a nice face, and a gentle voice. Just standing next to him made her feel protected, watched over. She eventually suggested they drive up the shoulder to the next exit. "We'd risk a ticket, I guess, but it's only about a mile up," she said.

"Sure, let's try it," he said. He figured they could be here forever, and he was tired and hungry, and this girl had eyes that seemed to illuminate the air around her. They got in their cars, she pulled ahead up the right shoulder, and he followed slowly along the gravelly pavement. She wasn't sure why she was taking this guy home. What if the old lady hears their cars pull in? What would Angela say to her? After a few minutes they were at her exit, which was nothing but the off-ramp and farmland. They drove a mile or so west on the dark country highway, turned into the stone driveway of a big old farmhouse, and parked alongside a small barn behind.

"This it?" Dan said as they got out of their cars, trying not to sound judgmental. "Kinda the middle of nowhere." He heard cows lowing in the distance, their pungent odor amplified by the day's heat, and he hoped it smelled better inside.

"Come on in," Angela smiled. "It's up here." She gestured to an outdoor staircase along the side of the barn, leading to a door. As they walked up the metal stairs a security light flickered on with a sickly blue glow. She watched the big house as she unlocked her door. Dan thought, despite the wave of heat crashing into him as they entered, it was surprisingly civilized inside, though it needed picking up. Living room, kitchenette with a small table and chairs. They took off their shoes, and she turned on the TV for light—a re-run of Wheel of Fortune on the all game-show channel.

"Sorry it's so stuffy," she said, switching on a window air conditioner. "I've been gone all day, and I don't like to leave windows open because..." she gestured outside.

"Cows," he said.

"Cows." She peeled off her socks, dropping them to the floor near her shoes.

"It's nice," he said.

"Rent's cheap," she said, getting two beers from the small fridge. She was so glad her brother keeps beer at her place for when he visits. "The couple in the big house have had the farm in their family for years and fixed-up this place for a little extra income." She sat next to him on the couch. They were quiet a minute.

Dan was starving. He used his shirt to wipe off the top of his beer and downed it quickly, feeling instantly tingly. A disturbingly chipper woman on TV spun a Bankrupt. Dan noticed, on Angela's feet, the wrinkly impressions left by her socks. A bit of white sock lint trapped at the corner of her big toenail. She could feel him gazing at her profile, hoping he hadn't noticed the collection of Disney videos on the shelf by the TV. Dan held up his empty bottle.

"Got another?" He asked. He decided to think she was a noble girl, giving up a nice apartment in a real town to look after some old couple.

"Sure. And are you hungry or anything, because I could…" She went to the kitchen, got two more beers and a can of Pringles. He tried not to rush, but ate most of the chips and drank the other beer quickly. He felt a little bad for using this nice girl. But then, maybe he'd see her again. This place was only thirty or forty miles from home. People date people from farther away than that, don't they? And when couples meet for the first time, it's not as if they *know* this is the night they'll be telling their grandchildren about someday—the night Grandpa figured he'd nail Grandma and ditch her, but then later discovered he might actually like her. This night could lead to something pretty cool, couldn't it?

Angela felt like they were only postponing the inevitable. Though she'd never done this kind of thing before, she knew she invited him back here to have sex with him. And she knew he must have assumed as much also. She drank her beer as fast as she could, telling herself it was for courage.

Near one a.m., after their third beers, a frozen pizza, and a Wheel marathon, he finally kissed her. Just turned to her, smiled, and kissed her. She was surprised, but also relieved it'd finally started. She drew his body up off the couch as they kissed, and he followed her to her bedroom. She kept the light off, and her t-shirt on, conscious of the foreign mass of her baby-weight body, leading him to the bed, feeling powerful and playful at the same time. Afterward they fell asleep in the pitch dark.

Dan woke at dawn's light glowing in the un-draped window, and it took a minute to remember where he was. He looked at Angela next to him. Then he spotted the empty baby crib in the corner of the room. He sat up, startled, a tide of guilt pulling at his gut. A kid? Where was it? What was a *mom* doing bringing strange men home?

As Dan peered down at Angela's limp, sleeping form—a bit fleshier than it had appeared to him only hours before—he was slightly horrified to see a blob of his own semen congealing on the back of her upper thigh. She slept soundly, oblivious to it, he thought, so she must lack nerve endings in that particular inch of her soft skin, an area that one would normally think would be quite sensitive to touch, especially the touch of a relative stranger's bodily fluids. And, he thought, if she was this insensitive, in what other areas of life might she be equally physically or emotionally ambivalent? The cries of pain from her newborn in her arms as she accidentally closes his toes in the kitchen drawer while retrieving an oven mitt? A spider dangling from the ceiling and landing on her head, disappearing into the auburn mass of her hair, perhaps deciding never to come out, pleased with its shiny henna-and-honey-scented home, retreating temporarily to the shelter of her ears when she showered?

Dan shuddered, rolling away from her. But it could be worse, maybe it wasn't a lack of nerve endings on her downy thigh skin that allowed her to sleep. Maybe she was simply able to ignore the semen because she was used to it. Because falling asleep with a strange man's cum smeared on her was a commonplace and therefore inconsequential occurrence. Could it be that he'd just ditched his friend on the highway to sleep with a woman for whom it was, in fact, *the norm* to doze soundly with a glob of foreign semen on her leg? Dan shuddered again, left the bed, showered thoroughly, borrowing her henna-and-honey-scented shampoo, washing his body with it because he refused to touch her bar of soap. When he finished, finding no clean towels in the bathroom cabinet, he shook his body like a dog, dripping all over her bathroom, though he now assumed she would neither notice nor care. He struggled his damp skin into his clothes, and he left.

As he walked to his car in the semi-dark of morning, he was glad he had not given her his phone number. Then he remembered the business card he'd given her back on I-75. He considered retrieving it, thinking she may have left it in her car, left the car unlocked since there wasn't a soul for miles—or, if it was locked, he could effortlessly, and quite like MacGyver, pick the lock with the prong of his belt buckle that he now realized he'd not even buckled in his haste to leave the squalor of her apartment. But instead he unlocked his own car door, with his key, and slumped into the seat.

He felt tired now, wanting to sleep, here in the violet morning with its barely lingering stars. Across a forlorn yard stood a monstrous oak, a plastic baby's swing suspended from a hefty branch. The swing swayed on its yellow nylon rope. A pink stroller stood on the back porch of the big farmhouse. Dan felt sick, as though he'd abetted a criminal, having encouraged a woman to abandon her baby with an old farmer's wife so he could screw her in the barn out back. Angela's face was a smudge in his mind. What color was her hair again? She was ruined—like a pot of leggy geraniums gone all to seed. Dan needed coffee. He drove off and phoned to wake up Craig.

As I re-filled their mugs, I heard Dan say, "…might not be so bad, you know."

I poured, then I pulled empty plates from 7 and 3. Stupid Dan—too afraid to even try. And I know even he's surprised at how quickly he got scared, and how he couldn't even think of some smooth way to ease himself out of the situation, couldn't avoid coming out of the whole think looking like a jerk. Poor Angela, I thought—waking from her first sound night's sleep in months to a headache, a condom oozing on the milk-crate nightstand, and guilt enough to drive a girl to church. She stashed the business card in her underwear drawer, peeks at it now and then.

Now that's something I have managed to keep control of —I don't screw strangers. Course, I've never met one I'd want to rush back to my apartment anyway. I guess I've thought about it, but I hate the idea of some strange man in my little home, looking at my photographs, pissing in my toilet, opening my fridge to ascertain the quality of what he finds inside.

Dan had fled from Angela's place like from a crime scene as soon as something took him by surprise, and now he couldn't erase all of the feelings he'd had for her up until then. He knew they were real—though that unique, late-at-night sort of real—and now he had to admit to himself that his ability to feel fear was more powerful than his ability to feel tenderness. It's better to avoid such situations altogether.

I mean, I've slept with guys, once I discovered I could get away with it, that mom wouldn't find out, wouldn't even try to find out. But none of the guys mattered. It's easier that way. No decisions, trying to figure out which feelings were real and which weren't. But I guess it would be nice if someone could matter. At least once. It sometimes worries me that I can't seem to let anyone matter, let them touch anything besides my plastic coating.

I asked 5 if they needed anything, dropped their check, pulled a plate. On the way to the dish room I overheard Meg inviting Lisa to go with her and Sandi to this bar to hear an Aerosmith cover band. She didn't bother to ask me because she knows I hate that kind of music.

Table #6

A woman, Lydia, walked past me, coming from the restrooms back to my eight-top, which she'd been holding for fifteen minutes, alone, waiting for people, sipping coffee. She's one of those hates-to-be-alone people. Fidgeting with her hair, stirring her mug, dabbing her mouth after each sip as though someone might catch her with a drip on her lip and scoff. Like anyone was really watching. She bugged me. She didn't even bring a magazine or anything, like there was no worthwhile way to pass the time if no one was with you, like she must have other people around for entertainment, for purpose.

Lydia checked her watch again, wondering where her husband, Ed, was and hoping he'd get there before his brother, Drew. She didn't want to be alone with Drew for long. Although she had nothing to do with his situation back then—hadn't even been dating Ed yet—she just couldn't forgive Drew for his ex-girlfriend's abortions. Twice. Twice he'd been able to convince his girlfriend to abort his baby. Every time she looked at him all she saw were those babies. Imagined them sinewy and bloodied and lying in a galvanized bucket in the corner of a fluorescent-lit, white-painted, room. Any time he mentioned money problems, Lydia had to bite her tongue to keep from saying, "Yeah, those clinics really gouge you, huh? But hey, at least there's no child support."

Ed knew how she felt, but it was years ago, and no one else in the family knew, and he told her to stay out of it. But when Drew recently got engaged, Lydia assumed Drew hadn't told his fiancée. She thought this girl deserved to know what he had done, and to decide for herself if she cared. The secret seethed in Lydia's gut whenever she saw the happy couple together. Ed encouraged her to try to get along with Drew and forget it. And they did get along fine at family gatherings and stuff. She was able to forget about the babies when there were enough distractions. She could laugh with them all, help Ed's mom mash the potatoes, have a pleasant meal, "Pass the gravy, Drew?" and listen to the guys talk football. Then out of nowhere Drew's face would suddenly appear completely cold to her, like any one of a hundred faces in a stranger's school yearbook, like the face of a man in a silent movie who you could tell, at first glance, was going to be the villain, the face of a man who needed everything to go his way.

As Ed got ready for work earlier this morning, Lydia told him, "Please don't be late this afternoon, OK?" She handed him his keys.

"Why? I mean, I won't, but…"

"Just… whatever. I'll see you at one o'clock." He agreed, kissed her forehead and left.

She moved to the window and watched the car drive down the rosy-lit street. The house was quiet. Closing her eyes, Lydia imagined for a moment the bustle of readying kids for school. Finding socks, stuffing brown lunch bags into backpacks, the youngest, maybe, not wanting to leave, saying, "wanna stay with Mommy!" She'd hug them all, sighing as they climbed into the bus with exaggerated huge steps, searching the row of small, smudged windows for their faces.

The rumble of a garbage truck snapped her eyes open. Her forehead was pressed against the window, slick with the warmth of her skin on the glass. She made coffee, the gurgles and drips resounding within the silent walls of the house.

Drew wasn't next to arrive at the café. It was Diane, Drew and Ed's sister, with her three-year-old, Tallie. Diane plunked a tote bag on the table and sighed. "I can't wait until preschool starts next fall."

"Tallie's so sweet, though." Lydia said, helping her into the chair next to her. Tallie kissed Lydia's cheek and began to stir nothing in a coffee mug. Lydia wondered if Drew's dead babies were girls or boys. And surely he'd have picked a better name than "Tallie." Maybe "Ed," after her husband.

I was named after my dad—well, my middle name, Ray. My mom feared she'd never have a boy, so she named me after Dad just to make sure she got it in there somewhere, figuring no one uses middle names anyway. For a while, while he was in the hospital, I started introducing myself to strangers as Ray. As a sort of tribute, I guess. Like it was my little sacrifice that somehow could make him pull through, the gods smiling down upon the tragic young girl with the boy's name who was soon to become fatherless. After he died, and I accepted that I hadn't found the secret Hoodoo cure for pancreatitis, I went back to being ashamed of my misnomer, hiding it again behind its initial. I guess Mom could have given me her name as my middle. Though our personalities are so dissimilar she probably would have asked me to change it by now.

It makes me wonder how she'd expected me to turn out. When she placed her hand on her belly, felt me thrashing inside, did she expect me to be a dentist when I grew up, or a poet, a governor? As all parents, I'm sure she wanted more for me than she had made of herself. Certainly she didn't dream of me waiting tables after college. "Oh, someday she'll pour coffee without spilling a drop, I just know it."

"So," Lydia said, looking at her watch. "Where is everyone?"

"I don't know—oh, here's Drew." Lydia looked up and saw Drew enter, a gust of warm air swirling in through the doors behind him. Ed followed a few steps behind. He kissed Lydia's forehead and sat.

"Tallie!" Drew smiled.

"Hi, Uncle D."

"Hey, after the wedding you can start on a few of these yourself," Diane said to Drew, stroking Tallie's hair.

"Oh, sure," Drew smiled, "We can't wait." Lydia felt a spasm in her throat and feared she might cry out. She clutched her mug and imagined splashing it in his face. Drew motioned to me for coffee. I brought the pots, poured for them, and left. Lydia had kept me waiting, and now they all had to wait because table 10 needed me.

Table #10

"You ready to order?" I poured Chris coffee then rested the pots on his table, pulled out my order pad.

"Sure," he said, reaching for sugar. "I'll have the Sunrise Special, over easy, bacon, white toast."

"Ok. Thanks," I reclaimed my coffee pots and left.

Chris is a guy we all want in our section. He's a guaranteed five bucks—too much, really, but that's just how he is. Money, for him, is a means to an immediate and pleasurable end. Last fall he was all flirty with Meg, always sat in her section, and started leaving her a ten each time. He is always attracted to girls with Meg's confident, semi-trampy looks and attitude. Girls who chomp gum, girls who dance alone alongside jukeboxes, girls who give him an excuse to indulge his vices.

"So are you gonna take me out sometime or what?" Meg eventually asked him, grinning at him from behind her order pad. They spent a lot of time at concerts and bars, staggering back to his cluttered apartment after last call. Things were nice for a couple of weeks or so—until he met Meg's sister, Heather, who she lived with. Chris adored Heather from first sight. She was so sweet, and demure—with her cotton cardigans and khaki pants—and smarter than Meg too, which was something he needed in a girl. Meg's no idiot, but Heather did Meg's taxes for her. Chris wanted to nuzzle Heather's round cheeks and unbutton her cardigan, slowly, slowly.

He started making excuses to stay in—which was good for him because he really couldn't afford to go out every night—so he could talk with Heather about movies and this fall's presidential race. Meg started to get bored.

"Want a beer, or are we going out?" she said one Thursday night as Chris helped Heather find the business section of the newspaper. Meg drank down half of a bottle in a few gulps.

"I was thinking," Chris said, trying to appear nonchalant, "maybe we could rent a DVD or something, or see what's on HBO."

"Whatever." Meg sighed. She came to the couch and sat on Chris's lap, drained the last of her beer, kissed his neck. He smelled her—musky perfume, hairspray, mixed with the beer and cigarettes on her breath. Drove him wild. Meg was hot. Long, deep-brown hair, glittery eyeshadow, and her teeth nipping at his ear. Chris grinned and kissed her, then suddenly stopped, embarrassed, remembering Heather in a chair next to them. "Come on," Meg said, leading him to her bedroom. "If we're not going out, let's at least get high."

As Meg passed him a joint he decided Heather was too good for him. Too nice. She was going to marry some former debate-team captain, some real-estate agent with his face on city bus-stop benches, a guy with more than two-hundred bucks in the bank. Sitting on the edge of Meg's unmade bed, he thought she's the type of girl who probably dates a lot of losers. He wondered if Heather thought he was just some loser too.

When his parents got divorced, and his mom left the house with her new boyfriend's Toyota running in the driveway, she gave him that telltale look, that look that even a twelve-year-old kid knows—she pitied him, she worried for him, she'd given up hope that he'd be anything more than he is right now.

That Thursday, after two joints, Chris slept with Meg then said, "Ya know, I kind of dig your sister." She kicked him out. He was genuinely surprised. "Hey!" he called to the closed door. "I still like you too!"

It reminds me of when I was a junior in high-school, and this guy from another school asked me to his prom. We'd only gone out a few times, but prom was getting close and his friends all had dates already. The week before the dance he went to Daytona Beach for Spring Break with some friends, and when he got back he told me he'd met a girl there who happened to live like ten miles from him back home in Toledo, and they had made out. "But I'll still take you to prom though," he said, like some kind of an Honorable Mention. What response did he want from me?

"No thanks," I told him. "Go ahead and take her."

"No, really," he said. "Thing is, I'd rather go with you. I love spending time with you, talking to you."

"What's that supposed to mean? Then why were you making out with some other girl if I'm so great?"

"I don't know." He said. At least he was honest. So I went to prom—hell I had the dress already—figuring it'd just be our last date. Our last, indescribably awkward date. There was a party at someone's house afterward, with a bunch of people I didn't know, our flouncy dresses and mussed chignons that looked festive in a gymnasium filled with helium balloons and disco balls were beginning to look ridiculous as we flopped on La-Z-Boys sucking Doritos residue from our fingers. I gradually got drunk on some syrupy concoction made with, among other things, Hawaiian Punch and rum, served from a stockpot nestled in the ice-filled kitchen sink. A gentle, rolling, thunderstorm blew by outside the crowded, lonely house of a stranger.

At two a.m. he and I lay flat on our backs, side by side in the darkened sunroom, listening to thunder, watching rain glazing in sheets down the walls of windows. "If only I could put your mind into her body, I'd have the perfect girl," he said.

"Nice." I felt like I was in a John Hughes movie.

"No, I mean that as a compliment," he squirmed.

"How the fuck is that supposed to be a compliment?" I didn't know whether to cry or backhand him.

"I mean, like, you have the perfect mind. Perfect for me, anyway."

"Just no tits and a boring face," I said. He didn't respond. He didn't need to. My brain accounted for half of a perfect girl. So what was the other half of me worth?

Now, I turned in Chris's order. Meg was whispering with Lisa by the hand sink, telling her about Chris, no doubt. Poor Chris. He just forgets sometimes that other people don't necessarily think the way he does. Other people think beyond the next few hours and like to prepare, however unconsciously, for the future. Other people would have anticipated that telling your girlfriend you dig her sister might cause some hurt feelings. Now, whenever he comes in, he assumes she's forgotten about him, like he's forgotten about her, waved off the unpleasantness and moved on to happier thoughts. He smiles at her, like he smiles at us all, leaves fives. I went back to the dining room to take the order at 6, turned it in, pulled plates from 9, brought syrup to 6, went to the kitchen for 10's plate, saw 4 was being seated.

Table #4

Two teenage girls sat down and ordered a stack of French toast to split, and coffees, lots of cream and sugar. Typical of girls their age—torn between their mind's desire to be bitter adults, and their body's desire for Hershey's syrup in milk.

The prettier girl, Emily, was training to be a lifeguard. She'd been swimming since she was an infant—her dad holding her tight, counting "one, two, three," then dunking her under water. Baby Emily never cried, didn't gasp for breath. Her mouth and nose didn't panic—they'd done their job of closing and remaining still. She never feared the water. But that wet infant didn't shout for joy either. She didn't clap and squeal, "Again, Daddy!" She merely accepted the ultra blue water over her head, around and through her eyelashes, lips, allowed it to swallow her as it may. By age three, she was diving off the high board and could swim breast or back stroke down the length of the pool. Her parents called her "Emmy Fish."

Emily's friend, Stacy, rented the Lincoln Club's pool after hours for her sixteenth birthday party. "Guess who's coming!" Stacy sing-songed to Emily at lunch at school.

"Who?" Emily grinned. Stacy paused dramatically, chewing a bite of granola bar. "Who?"

"Oh, just Shawn Kusinski," Stacy said.

"No way!" Emily darted her eyes side to side, lowered her voice. "For sure?"

"He's coming with Todd and Brad and those guys. He told me." The guys were all Seniors, and Emily began mentally preparing for them, for the party, as she sipped her 7up. Should she curl her hair or clip it up? Which would make her look older? Her pink sundress made her look taller, but her yellow one matched her bikini.

"What should I wear?" Emily said, half to herself.

"You should borrow my gold sandals—the ones with the glitter. With your yellow dress," Stacy said. Emily smiled but felt a bit dazed as the bell rang and she stood to leave the lunchroom. They pushed through the clogged hallway.

"I can't believe I finally get a chance to hang out with Shawn," Emily said. Shawn, who is able to make the teachers laugh in spite of themselves. Shawn, with eyes like the deep end. Shawn, who can draw really well—though he doesn't make a big deal of it—and Emily knows because his still-life of a conch shell and cattails hung six steps from her locker during the winter art fair, and each time she passed it she couldn't help but trail her fingertip along the lower edge of the paper, where his first name was written in tiny block letters.

"I've done my part," Stacy said. "Now you just have to loosen up and *talk* to the guy." Emily dropped her head. "I mean, he's like, just a guy."

"I know. Later." Emily kept walking as Stacy slipped in to her Algebra class. It stung Emily to hear Stacy call her out on her shyness. Emily'd always been this way and she thought her best friend should find it an endearing quality, not tell her just to grow up and get over it. It wasn't that simple.

I remember feeling the same way Emily feels in school. Walking through the bustling hallway, getting dizzy from other people's conversations. All of their giggles and shouts and plans for the weekend swirling in our ears like white noise. There's so much life, so much love, between friends—boyfriends, girlfriends, couples. Why can't everyone just shut up? And why must people be forever touching, shoulders mashing together in the halls, arms jerking awkwardly outward and bumping elbows, heads?

The night of the party, Emily was giddy. She'd bought Stacy a CD, Madonna's Immaculate Collection, and they popped it in. Stacy had hung strings of Christmas lights along the check-in office and clubhouse, and Emily wondered how they'd look from just under the surface of the water. The pool felt like a second home to Emily. She knew where there was a crack in the concrete that ran from the deep-end ladder right to the check-in counter. She'd stuck a blob of blue gum under the central lifeguard platform three summers ago and it was still there. She checked each time she walked by. She remembered when they'd planted the redbud trees along the west and east fences—now they were taller than the clubhouse. But of course it was the water that she came for. For hours on end she'd dive, or swim laps, or just float and imagine she was drifting out to sea with miles and miles of buoyant life below her.

Shawn came late, after they'd already cut the cake, and Emily had frosting on her mouth when he walked in. She frantically wiped it off and hoped he wouldn't talk to her yet— she wasn't ready. He sat on the edge of the pool, his feet dangling in, eating a piece of cake from his hand. She wondered how he wanted her to act. Should she do something brazen, like sit beside him and ask for a bite of his cake, or should she sneak up and push him in the pool? And if he couldn't swim, she could dive in and rescue him, tug his large body, almost weightless under the dark water, his arms reaching around her waist, clasping to her, grateful for the thrill of nearly drowning in her arms. Or would that piss him off?

I never knew how to act around boys when I was her age. I guess no girl does. But the difference was I didn't care that much. I guess I accepted the fact that I was never going to be a perfect match for anyone else, so why try? I might just as well try to speak Cantonese. It just wasn't happening. I remember being at a friend's house once when she had a babysitter. A high-school guy—very cute, nice guy, seemed bored to be stuck with a couple of ten-year-olds. My friend flirted with him endlessly, and pointlessly, considering he was at least five years older than us, which at that age was a lifetime. Still, she wouldn't drink her Coke because it would smudge her raspberry lip gloss, asked him how many push-ups he could do.

She put her parents' jazz tapes in the stereo, twirling and waggling around the living room, tugging on my arms to pull me off the couch to dance too, but I wouldn't because I knew how foolish and decidedly non-tantalizing she looked. Some people would give her credit for trying, but I found the futility of the trying to be merely pathetic. It's best to know when to concede.

Emily opted to swim. She walked to the high dive just as "Like a Prayer" was starting. Looking down at the water, lit from within by yellowy spotlights, she felt at home. She knew how it would feel on her skin, rushing over her, holding her as she sliced through it, and how her body would look from above as she glided along the bottom to re-surface on the opposite side. She dove and was at peace in the muffled, cool world.

When she climbed up the ladder she remembered Shawn and looked to see if he'd watched her. He was throwing water balloons at Stacy and Todd by the food table. One burst at Stacy's feet and she feigned panic, running for a towel. Shawn ran after her, smashing a balloon on her back. She shrieked. Shawn helped gently towel her dry, laughing. Emily couldn't help wondering if she would be the one Shawn was softly stroking if only she was playing around with them all. As great-looking as he was, she couldn't really imagine him touching her.

"Nice dive." It was Brad, sitting on a chaise by the ladder.

"Thanks." Brad handed her his towel. Black with sailboats on it. It was warm, and not until she wrapped it around her did she realize she'd felt cold.

"Thirsty?" Brad asked.

"Sure." She wondered what it was about Brad that made him want to talk to her. Guys didn't ever just walk right up to her. Something about her warded them off. But whatever it was, he was immune to it. They walked to the large plastic tub filled with ice and cans of soda. He plunged his arms into the icy water, wincing, and produced two Cokes. "Thanks." His can fizzed when he opened it and foam dribbled down his arm. She watched him lick the length of his forearm, laugh, and wipe his mouth of the back of his hand.

She'd seen Brad in school—she passed him every day as she left the Biology lab and he came in for the next period—but she'd never paid him much attention. Now she had a rush of excitement, like she'd just been whispered a secret. She wanted him to be in the water with her.

"Let's all play volleyball!" Stacy announced, Shawn's arm draped over her shoulder, and everyone ambled through the gate and down the sloping lawn to the sand court. Brad began to walk away.

"Hey," Emily blurted, "let's swim instead."

"Ok." Brad took her Coke and set them down. They jumped in the shallow end. The water felt warm as the night air cooled, and it enveloped her like a sleeping bag. She didn't know what to say, what he'd want to talk about. "Hey, dive for me again?" he said.

"Ok," Emily smiled. She knew she dove well. They swam to the deep end, and she climbed up the ladder. "Ready?" she called. Brad waved. She hopped twice and dove, the spring-rattle resonating in the night. Her fingers sliced a path for her body in the blue-black. When they touched bottom, she curved and propelled herself upward, her head swollen with cool pressure, kicking her body towards the ladder and Brad's legs. She grabbed his feet from under the water, climbed hand-over-hand up to his waist, his muscles flexing to keep himself afloat. She held tight and bobbed her head above the water. She let it stream down her face. Brad's eyes were wide. "Nice?" she said.

"Nice." Brad looked at her. The Madonna CD ended and clicked itself silent. They each steadied themselves with one hand on the ladder, and he pulled her toward him with his free hand. He kissed her, and she felt an urgent need to go under water, kicking, reminding herself that she was already mostly submerged. Brad fumbled to get his hand under her wet bikini top, and she could feel his stiffened penis within his swim trunks as he pressed against her. Her eyes opened wide and she saw his were closed. She watched his face—lost, like a drowning man—and allowed him to slide against her, listening to the other kids cheering at volleyball beyond the fence, the water lapping at the pool corners, washing over his shoulders, neck, his gaping mouth.

He suddenly jerked, his chin jutting forward, his hand squeezing her arm very tightly, and Emily wasn't certain what had happened, only that as soon as it started it stopped, and he relaxed. He held her a moment, panting into her ear, then quietly climbed the ladder. He wrapped in his towel, sat sipping his Coke. Emily took a breath and slipped under the water. She walked her hands down the pool wall, feeling the domed cover of a golden light. Her legs floated. The water knew her. It forgave.

"Girls," I asked as I passed by, "you need more cream?"

"Sure, thanks," Emily said sweetly. The table was littered with empty sugar packets. They seemed to enjoy stirring, clinking their mugs with their spoons in circles. Talking intently, sharing. I brought a cream pitcher and refilled their glasses of water.

They enjoyed thinking they were almost grown up. That's probably why the teen-aged years are so wonderful. Because you're gaining independence—driving, thinking about college and getting the hell out of your parents' house, and all that—but you still can hide behind your youth. In the back of your mind you know if you screw up you're not really accountable. After all, you're just a kid. You can act stupid with your friends, do the stuff now that you figure you'll have to give up once you become a "responsible adult." Like watching cartoons, or getting drunk at a friend's house and sleeping over in their bed with them, or blowing bubbles with your gum. It's your last chance to be an idiot, and have your idiocy automatically excused. Maybe that's why I hate teenagers. They flaunt their power, ooze indestructible youth, thinking we're all jealous.

But they're wrong after all. They don't realize that, in truth, they can still do whatever the hell they want when they're adults. I mean, no one pays attention to what other people are doing, or knows who other people really are. We don't know what's going on in their kitchens, their cars, or their heads. We just use their lives to affect our own—whatever it takes to keep going.

I brought the check to Chris at 10, asked if he needed anything more, then I went to the kitchen for a drink of water before 6's food came up on the line. Meg was just coming in from a smoke break. "Hey," she said, re-applying lipstick, "you ok?"

"Fine," I said, filling a Styrofoam cup from the tap. I was waiting for her to ask me what I was doing this weekend. Trying to think of an excuse not to go out with her. "I'm fine. I…"

"Hmm?"

"I just hate people sometimes," I said, sipping.

"Hell, you need a different job then," Meg laughed, heading to the floor.

I sat a moment and watched Rusty. His feet sprung back and forth in tiny, bouncy steps as he turned his body from grill to line, grill to line, preparing food. He joked easily with the other line cook and the prep guy who'd just started last month. He smiled and talked and his arms swung from orderly rows of pancakes on the grill, to trays of omelet fillings, to pans of eggs sizzling on the grill, back to flip-flip-flip the pancakes, back to the omelet pans. What struck me was that his brain was able to disassociate from his work. As if he could work a whole shift and have no idea what he'd made—though it'd all be made perfectly. But he would remember what he'd talked about—how the prep guy suspects his girlfriend might be cheating on him with a guy at her bank, how the busser got screwed on a brake job, how his wife's been shopping for bunk beds for the kids to make room for the baby due winter. Rusty manages to have a life that not only continues despite his work, but seems to glow by comparison. I have nothing beyond these greasy walls.

In the afternoon, when my last table left, I went to the dry storage room for a box of Sweet-and-Low to re-stock the front line. In the back hall I could see Meg and Lisa's backs as they disappeared into the office. I grabbed a small box, a big bag of straws. I could hear Lisa's voice low though the wall, couldn't tell what she was saying. "I guess," I heard Meg say. "Nobody really knows her."

I remembered how, when I'd gone camping with Meg and Sandi and her boyfriend, I'd wanted them to like me. I remember staring into the fire, needing to pee, afraid if I left them I'd disappear. But I stumbled toward the brush, over the uneven ground to the water's edge. I pulled my jeans all the way off, squatted and peed right into the bay, the rippling waves lapping it all away.

Squatting there I remembered when I was ten, on a car-trip with my family, and we pulled over in a cornfield so my sister and I could pee. We ran, laughing, from the car, and when we were hidden, peeing safely behind the stalks, I saw my sister pull out a little silver flask from her jacket pocket. She snuck a swallow, and we went back to the car. I had thought, then, how big that cornfield seemed, like we could run through it straight to the ocean. I had thought how crazy my sister was, but always, always smiling.

In the dark, hearing Meg and Sandi laughing behind me, I wanted to get in that water, wanted it to hold me, suspended. I tugged off the rest of my clothes, slipped in, heard the others laughing, following me into the water. My eyes wouldn't focus. All I saw was one fleshy smear after another bobbing up out of the water. I felt the coolness of the water leeching up under my plastic coating, loosening it. I imagined it peeling away, like cellophane, and floating out, becoming an invisible part of the water, sinking to the bottom with the rocks and fish. I was afraid to move, afraid it might re-stick and never peel away again. I floated, hidden under the black water, my feet suspended above the rocky ground, feeling the drifting and sinking of the plastic.

From the storage room, I decided to grab a case of napkins too, a box of herbal teabags, a packet of coffee filters, and I stuffed my pockets with the last in a case of slender Tabasco bottles, kicking the empty box to the floor, stomping it flat. I stocked the front line really full, so it wouldn't need anything from anyone for a long time.

Acknowledgments

The author wishes to thank the editors of *Anti-Heroin Chic* in which a different version of a passage in this book first appeared (2021)

Kerry is also grateful to Jason Baldinger for the use of his lovely photographs, and to Katie Schmeling for her thoughtful and assiduous editing.

Kerry's Favorite Restaurants

Kerry's favorite restaurants are/were:

- Kewpee Hamburgers (Lima, OH)
- Dominic's & Carlita's (Toledo, OH)
- Cafe Marie (Toledo, OH)
- Sam & Andy's Uptown Cafe (Toledo, OH)
- Frisch's Big Boy (Toledo,OH)
- Scramblers (Findlay, OH)
- Birds (Los Angeles, CA)
- Berardi's (Sandusky, OH)
- Westway Diner (New York, NY)

About the Author

Kerry Trautman is a lifelong Ohioan. Her poetry and fiction have appeared in numerous journals, and in anthologies such as *Mourning Sickness* (Omniarts, 2008); *Delirious: A Poetic Celebration of Prince* (NightBallet Press, 2016); *Nine Lives Later: A Dead Cat Anthology* (Dee Dee Chapman, ed., 2017); *The Secrets We Keep* (Dandelion Revolution Press, 2021); and *Let Me Say This: A Dolly Parton Poetry Anthology* (Madville Publishing, 2023). Her poetry books are *Things That Come in Boxes* (King Craft Press, 2012); *To Have Hoped* (Finishing Line Press, 2015); *Artifacts* (NightBallet Press, 2017); *To be Nonchalantly Alive* (Kelsay Books, 2020); *Marilyn: Self-Portrait, Oil on Canvas* (Gutter Snob Books, 2022); and *Unknowable Things* (Roadside Press, 2023).